This book belongs to

For Sterling,
a boy of few words who can light up
my world with his incredible laugh.

Santa's Lost Reindeer
Copyright © 2021 Spirit Frog Press

Illustrations by Ramesh Ram
Cover Design by Melinda Martin
Formatted by Praise Saflor

Publisher's Cataloging-in-Publication data

Names: Hilz, Rachel, author. | Ramesh, Ram, illustrator.
Title: Santa's lost reindeer / written by Rachel Hilz; illustrated by Ram Ramesh.
Description: Vancouver, BC Canada: Spirit Frog Press, 2021. |
Summary: How can Christmas be saved? Santa's in so much trouble. With his
best reindeer missing, he needs help – on the double!
Identifiers: ISBN: 978-1-7772619-5-5 (hardcover) |
978-1-7772619-4-8 (paperback) | 978-1-7772619-6-2 (ebook)
Subjects: LCSH Reindeer--Juvenile fiction. | Santa Claus--Juvenile fiction. |
Christmas--Juvenile fiction. | BISAC JUVENILE FICTION / Animals / Deer, Moose
& Caribou | JUVENILE FICTION / Holidays & Celebrations / Christmas & Advent |
JUVENILE FICTION / Humorous Stories
Classification: LCC PZ7.1.H5665 San 2021 | DDC [E]--dc23

Santa's Lost Reindeer

Rachel Hilz

Remesh Ram

'Twas the night before Christmas...the night just before, when good ol' Saint Nicholas showed up at my door.

He knocked and he knocked, then pounded and pounded, that jolly old man with a belly so rounded...

from cookies and milk and all sorts of goodies,
that he gobbled down quickly while warming his footies.

He flung the door open, bashed into the wall,
and there Santa stood, trying hard not to fall.

He was gasping for breath and gripping the wall.
"That new reindeer's the one who's to blame for it all.

That foolish deer fled. He was spooked by a jet.
I'm sorry to say I'm just very upset."

"And to my dismay, I just have to say,
that even ol' Santa can have a bad day."

"I'm training new deer. See, my last team got old.
They said they were tired. They said they were cold.

They said their backs ached and their eyesight was failing.
They griped and they grumbled because they were ailing."

"But we lost this new guy
when our sled took a dive.
Now I need some real help
from a big four-wheel drive."

"I'm afraid Bucky's lost somewhere out in the cold,
and for tracking down reindeer, I'm getting too old.

I was hoping you'd help me to find my large pet.
There are many deliveries we haven't made yet.

I'm afraid he's still learning and might be in trouble.
I must hurry to find him, so... Quick!

On the

double!"

So the rest of us climbed in the truck super quick.
There was Mom, and myself, and good ol' Saint Nick.

Inside our garage,
       the eight reindeer stayed warm,
while we all froze our bums
       in a giant snow storm.

Santa said, "We will find him, even though it is night.
After all, on the end of his nose is a light!"

We went to find Bucky, with his bright yellow glow.
We hoped it would shine through the blizzarding snow.

We traveled for miles on the slick winter road.
It was snowing and blowing, and ever so cold.

Then we finally saw, through the black of the night,
a set of great antlers and a shining, bright light.

There stood our poor Bucky, incredibly lost,
and so cold that his coat was all covered with frost.

Santa stepped from the truck onto white, crispy snow.
He said, "Oh! I'm so glad to see Bucky's bright glow."

But Bucky was cold, frozen right to the bone.
"We must warm him," Mom said. "Then let's get him home."

So into the truck went the frozen reindeer,
while down Santa's cheek slid a warm, joyful tear.

We took Bucky home
and thawed him right out,
then Santa's team left
to continue their route.

Before Santa left, as he started to go,
he looked at me, saying, "I want you to know...
I really love Bucky. He's such a good deer.
When he disappeared, I had so much to fear!"

"I think Bucky's happy to give me a scare.
If a deer has nine lives, he's got no more to spare.
Thank you for helping me find him tonight.
Thank you for helping make everything right."

Santa stopped and he paused. He said nothing more.
He walked right on past me and rushed out the door.

Then as quick as he left, he came running back in...
with presents piled all the way up to his chin.

Santa carried the presents to our Christmas tree,
and spread them all out for my family and me.

The time had then come for ol' Santa to go.
He headed outside into white, swirling snow.

Then into the night, Santa left with his deer.
"Merry Christmas to all!" was what I could hear.

I stared up at the sky on that dark, snowy night...
I saw it! Oh, yes! There goes Bucky's bright light!

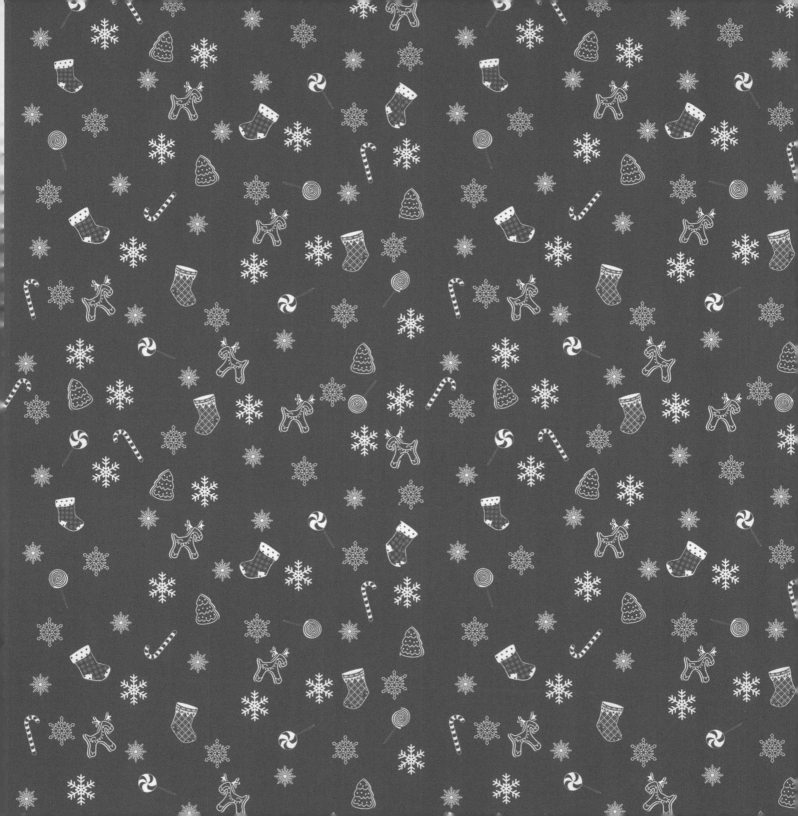